REAL-LIFE
SCARY
KIDS

BY TRACEY E. DILS

cover illustration by Bill Schmidt
interior illustrations by Bob Carter

To Emily Nelle Herrold, my spirited daughter

⩗PAGES™

First printing by Willowisp Press 1997.

Published by Willowisp Press
801 94th Avenue North, St. Petersburg, Florida 33702

Printed in the United States of America

2 4 6 8 10 9 7 5 3 1

ISBN 0-87406-854-1

contents

A GHOSTLY WELCOME!

Could This Happen To You?

You're enjoying a pleasant summer afternoon, when you notice your older sister walking through the garden. Only it's not exactly your sister. How do you know? When you reach for her hand, your hand goes completely through hers!

Or . . .

You're minding your own business in your own home, when suddenly things begin flying around the room. And then something more terrifying happens! You suddenly feel an invisible claw scratching deeply into the flesh of your face.

Or . . .

You feel mysteriously drawn to a book at your local library and you take it home without checking it out. Later that night, someone—or something—comes to demand that you take the book back. Or else!

Or . . .

You travel into the Texas wilderness to hunt wild boars and find yourself hunted by something much fiercer—a creature who is half-girl and half-wolf. And, even more frightening, she may be a half-human, half-animal ghost!

These stories sound incredible, but they are really "true" ghost stories. And what makes them even more terrifying is that they happened to kids just like you.

Are they really ghosts? Do they haunt kids? Are ghost stories really true?

These are questions that you, the reader,

need to decide for yourself. What is true about these stories is that someone—usually more than one person—claims to have experienced the events firsthand. These people have written down the details so that others could help them make sense of what happened. Their factual accounts of what happened are what inspired the terrifying tales in this collection.

I have a special job as a writer of "real-life" scary stories. That job starts when I research the actual scary event to find out what the "real" facts are. But it doesn't end there. My job, first and foremost, is to tell the best and scariest story I can. I have stayed true to the basic facts of the story, but where details were missing, I filled them in from my own imagination. That means taking those facts and weaving them into a terrifying tale—with a beginning, a middle, and an end.

And now it's time to stretch your imagination. You've probably heard about ghostly encounters in your own community or in your family. Try taking the basic facts of the encounter and turn them into a story, one with a beginning, a middle, and an end. And remember that kids love to hear stories about kids like themselves. So, if your stories involve "real-life scary kids," they're sure to be extra-frightening to your friends and family.

And, as you read these ghost stories or create some of your own, remember—when you write ghost stories, you're joining a special group of writers whose main goal is to frighten readers as much as possible. Edgar Allan Poe is considered to be the master scary story teller, but there are other great writers, like Mary Shelley and Washington Irving, who also tried their hand at scary tales. If you're interested in learning more about how ghost stories work or in writing them yourself, take a look at the terrifying tales these great writers created. Who knows? You may invent a scary tale that will rival theirs!

But for now, sit back, relax, and turn to the first story in the book. And be prepared to feel a chill in the air. There's nothing scarier than a story about a haunted kid—a kid who was just like you!

THE TERROR OF THE MURDERED PRINCES

*E*NGLAND'S *history is full of grisly murders—
many of them in the royal family itself. Some
of the murders were carried out in secret, and
we're only today learning the full details. Others
were public executions. Queens, princes,
princesses, and other royal servants were each
accused of some petty crime and were
imprisoned in the Tower of London. And then,
although they were probably innocent, each one
was found guilty by a judge and sentenced to*

death—usually by having his or her head chopped off by a sword.

In almost every case, there was one reason that these royal figures were killed—power. Those who were executed had power, and they were killed so the murderers could achieve their own royal status. Perhaps the most tragic of all these murders happened in England in 1483. It was here that a young prince who was destined to be king and his younger brother were brutally murdered at the hands of an unlikely criminal— their own uncle, the boys' guardian. The murder went unsolved for over two hundred years, until one day when the boys' ghosts returned to set the record straight.

The time is the late 1600s and the Tower of London needed some work. James didn't mind hard work—he liked it, especially when it came to building things. That's why he was thrilled when he was selected to work on rebuilding and enlarging one part of the Tower. It was the kind of work he loved best—as long as he didn't have to do it alone.

James's fellow workers didn't blame him for his feelings. None of them liked to work alone in the Tower either. After all, the fortress had a long history of violence and terror. Inside its stone walls, hundreds of people had met their bloody end. Most were first imprisoned in tiny, cold rooms. And then, when their time came, they were led to the courtyard to be beheaded. James knew that most of the Tower's victims were not an ordinary kind of criminal. They were often royalty or members of the king's court. For some reason, they had fallen into disfavor or had committed some crime against the kingdom of England. Once inside the thick walls of the Tower, their bloody fate was usually permanently sealed. The Tower of London, James knew, was the bloodiest place in all of England's history.

James also knew that some claimed that the ghosts of the Tower's victims still walked its hallways, crying for mercy, which is why he didn't like working alone. James had heard that several of the guards had actually seen the ghost of Anne Boleyn, one of King Henry VIII's wives, roaming the Tower. The guards said the ghost didn't have a head, just a bloody stump where the head had been.

And some of the workmen had claimed to hear bloodcurdling screams in the late afternoons. It was rumored that the screams came from the ghost of Guy Fawkes, a commoner who had tried to blow up the Houses of Parliament, the governing body of England. He had been tortured almost to death in the Tower before his beheading.

But as long as James worked side-by-side with the other workers, he was able to forget the stories of the hauntings and the Tower's hideous history. With a companion nearby, he could focus on the task at hand.

One afternoon, though, James remembered that he had left some tools in one of the rooms in the Tower. The other workmen were all packing to leave, and James didn't have the heart to interrupt them. After all, the renovations were almost finished. And James hadn't heard of anything particularly haunting in this room. So he swallowed hard and went to the room where he had left his gear.

As James climbed the stairs, he couldn't get over the feeling that he was being followed by someone. He even thought he heard footsteps behind him, but when he turned around, no one was there. *Just my imagination,* he thought, as he continued to climb the cold, wooden stairs.

When he reached the top, he took a deep breath and reached for the door. Then he gasped.

The door was swinging open as if someone was pushing it. He turned to run back down the steps, but something seemed to be blocking his way, making it impossible for him to go back to where his companions were waiting.

Then he felt himself being turned back toward the room. He tried desperately to push away from the invisible force that was holding him in its grip, but it was impossible.

James stared straight ahead into the room. There, huddled in the corner, were two small boys. They looked to be about ten and twelve years old. They were dressed in nightgowns of rich silk. Their hair was cut in a style that seemed strange to James, straight and long. And they clung to each other's hands as if they were hanging on for dear life.

But it was the look on their faces that impressed James most of all. Their faces held a terror that James had never seen before. They looked frightened—terrified for their lives. Their eyes were red and bloodshot, their mouths were twisted in a strange grimace, and their skin had a white pallor. It was a look of terror and agony. And it was a look that made James's own blood chill in his veins.

Then, suddenly, James heard a popping sound, and the two boys disappeared. The force that had once held tightly to James's own shoulders released him, and he fell to the ground. He stood up quickly and shook himself. He must have been seeing things—and feeling things. This couldn't have happened. It just seemed too strange.

James turned and ran down the steps of the Tower to find his friends, but the other workmen were no longer busily preparing to leave. They were huddled around a wooden box, a crate of some kind. One claimed that he had found the crate underneath the staircase James had just climbed.

"We should open it!" one said.

"There are probably jewels hidden inside. Why else would it have been hidden in that compartment in the wall?"

"Nay," said another. "It is royal property—

just like the Crown Jewels that are kept in the Throne Room."

"But we found it," said another. "We ought to at least see what is inside."

Suddenly, James heard his own voice command, "Open it. Open it *now*." For some reason, he was desperate to see what was inside.

The tone of James's voice must have convinced his companion, because he took his hammer and pried the wooden case open. As he peered inside, he let out a strange moan.

James pushed the small crowd aside so he could see for himself what was in the box. He, too, cried out in terror when he saw its contents.

There were two skeletons inside the box, and they were exactly the size of the young boys whom he had seen in the room upstairs. The skeletons were dressed in long, silk night-gowns—the same ones he had seen on the boys just moments earlier. And, even in death, their bony hands were entwined. Once again, the blood in his veins ran cold.

"It's the young princes," one of the workers was saying. "We've found them after all these years."

"The princes?" James asked, feeling his heart beating in his chest. "Tell me more."

"You must have heard of the princes—you know, Edward V and his brother Richard, the Duke of York. They had been imprisoned in one of these rooms by their uncle, the Duke of Gloucester. The Duke was a wicked one, he was. He had wanted the boys out of the way so he could take over the throne and become king."

James nodded his head in slow recognition. He remembered the story now. The boys had simply disappeared. There had been rumors, of course, that they had been brutally murdered one night and that the Duke himself had ordered the killings. And the Duke *had* gone on to take over the throne as King Richard III.

Once again, he heard his voice speaking, as if he had no control over it.

"Bury the bones," he said.

"Huh?" one of his friends asked.

"Bury the bones. They need to be buried—a proper royal burial. That's what the boys want. That is what the king must do."

The very next day, King Charles II had the bones blessed and buried in a ceremony worthy of the young princes. James and the rest of the workmen went on to finish their work in the Tower.

And, while other phantoms still walk the halls of the Tower of London, no one ever again saw the ghosts of the princes. They seemed to have come back to demand their royal rights— even after their own grisly murders.

THE BLOODY REVENGE OF THE SERVANT BOY

*R*EVENGE. There is perhaps no stronger motivation for violence and retribution. And when someone has been wrongly accused—especially a young person—the need for revenge seems powerful enough to transcend the grave itself.

And so it was with young Richard, a servant who lived in England in the 1700s. He was innocent of the crimes of which he was accused—and he would do anything, even come back

25

from the dead, to prove it.

George had only been in London a few weeks when he received an urgent message from his butler, Morris, who had been managing his estate while he was away. He had to come home at once, Morris's letter read.

George wasn't sure what it was about, but he was certain that Morris wouldn't have sent him the message without good reason. After all, he was serving on King George II's court in the early 1700s. One wasn't asked to leave such a post without good reason. After getting permission to go, George hurried home to his estate in Exeter in Devon County, England.

Morris, a bit breathless, met him at the door. "It was Tarwell, sir, Richard Tarwell and his band of hooligans. They broke in and tied me up and . . ."

"Hold on," George said. "Slow down. Tied you up, you say? Young Richard? He is but fourteen years old."

Morris nodded and continued with a tale of unbelievable treachery. According to Morris, Richard Tarwell, the young servant boy whom George had hired just before he left, willingly let a band of highwaymen into the house. They walked right into the pantry and began dumping the silver into their bags. When Morris discovered them in the act, they tied him up. Tarwell had been the one to bind his hands, he insisted. Then they headed off into the night and had not been seen since.

George shook his head in disbelief. He could believe the part about the highwaymen. They had been a menace to this part of England lately. But he couldn't figure out why Richard would join them. He had known Richard since he was a child. Richard's father had worked in George's stables for years. And Richard himself was a fine young man. He had become like a son to George. George had even given him a special knife with a pearl handle and silver blade that had been in his family for years.

"Are you sure? You're sure Richard was involved?"

"Aye," Morris replied. "He opened the door for them and then joined in. It was as if he had known them a long time."

It still didn't sound like something Richard would do. When George questioned Richard's father, he insisted that Richard was innocent.

27

His son would never be involved in something like this. He knew Richard respected George and appreciated the kindness he had shown him.

But there seemed to be no other explanation. The silver was gone and so was Richard. It seemed that everyone must have misjudged the young man. He must have been a criminal after all.

Those thoughts were still with George as he bedded down for the night. It was as if he was having a kind of strange argument with himself—one side said that Richard had to be innocent, but the other side insisted that he was guilty of the crime. After all, the evidence certainly pointed toward Richard's guilt, and Morris wasn't known to be a liar. George drifted off into a troubled sleep, trying to make sense of all that had happened.

In the middle of the night, George suddenly awoke. A candle was lit beside his bed and, in the glow of its light, he could see a figure—a figure of a young man who looked just like Richard Tarwell. And in his hand was a knife, the pearl-handled knife that George himself had given him.

"Richard!" he shouted. "I knew you'd come back. Now you can tell me just what happened!"

The figure didn't speak. It simply smiled and beckoned. And as it did, George could tell that it wasn't a person at all, but a cloudy image.

His heart began to pound and he could hear the blood rushing in his ears, but he couldn't stop himself. For some strange reason, his body seemed pulled out of the bed and toward the apparition. He paused just a second to throw a cloak over his bedclothes, and then he followed the figure downstairs and out the front door.

The figure led him to a large elm tree about a half-mile from the house. The bottom of the elm was surrounded by thick bushes, many with sharp thorns. The whitish figure used the knife to point to the ground at the base of the tree.

"What is it, Richard? Can you tell me what is there?"

He was greeted with silence. The apparition just kept pointing, this time with more in-sistence, jabbing at the darkness with the silver knife.

Then George felt a cold breeze on his neck

and the figure of Richard Tarwell seemed to fade before his eyes.

George stared at the tree for a moment and he then turned and headed back into the house. *Perhaps this is all some sort of strange dream,* he told himself as he climbed the stairs. *I'll probably wake up soon and it will be as if it never happened.*

But when George woke up that morning, he was convinced that he had seen Richard Tarwell's ghost. Whether it was a dream or not, Richard was trying to tell him something, he was sure of it. And that something had to do with that tree.

He ordered his gardener to dig up the area around the tree, a project that took well into the afternoon because of the thorny bushes that surrounded it. He had wanted to talk to Morris about it, to get the butler's story once again, but it was his day off and he had gone to his family's cottage in the next town. So George just sat and watched as the gardener dug and dug.

Finally, the gardener let out a horrified shout.

"It's young Richard's coat!" he said. "He must have buried it here. But why?"

But George knew they would find much more than Richard's coat. He joined the gardener in his digging, furiously throwing one shovelful after another over his shoulder.

Then he hit something hard. It wasn't just Richard's coat. It was the body of Richard himself. As they pulled his twisted body from the ground, it became more and more obvious what had happened. He had been murdered, his throat cut savagely. If Richard had been part of this evil crime, he had been killed by the other criminals. And they had absconded with the rest of the silver.

George knew he had to find out the truth and to do that, he had to find Morris. Morris could tell him the story again, and maybe he would hear something different, something that would make it clear exactly what had happened.

He summoned his horses and took off toward the town where Morris had gone. He headed to the cottage that Morris had described to him so many times before.

When he knocked on the door, no one answered. He knocked again, and then pushed the heavy door aside.

He gasped at what he saw. There, on the rough wooden table just inside the door, was his stolen silver. Morris had taken it! And he had hidden it here. He must have killed young Richard, too.

What George saw next turned his gasp into a scream.

On the floor, just beyond the table, lay Morris himself. His throat had been slit from one side to another. Blood still dripped from the wound. It seemed as if Morris had been so ashamed of his deed that he had taken his own life rather than face the consequences.

But when George looked closer, he saw something that made him tremble with fear. It was the silver knife, the one with the pearl handle, the one that had been in his family for years. The one he had given to Richard. Then he remembered that this was the very knife that had appeared in his dream.

Now George knew another truth. Something far different and more horrifying had occurred in that room.

The ghost of Richard Tarwell, the wrongly accused servant boy, had avenged the crime of the stolen silver and of his own bloody murder.

THE
GHOST
OF THE
SPANISH
MAIDEN

*L*OVE has inspired great poetry, beautiful music, and magnificent art work. Love has also caused painful heartbreak, heartbreak that sometimes has led to desperate acts—even murder.

The love of one John Robinson for a young and beautiful Spanish girl may have been the kind of desperate love that brought Robinson to such an unspeakable act. But before he actually performed his bloody work, he left behind an *incredible creation, one that was a fitting testament to the young beauty he loved so much. But she had her own desperate love— and it was this love that kept her spirit alive, even though her body had died.*

He was a strange one, that old John Robinson. Everyone in the small town of Delaware, Ohio, agreed about that much. He had appeared suddenly in the area. Some said he came to the area from the East, on foot. Others said he came down from Canada where he had been trapping and trading with the Indians. There were even rumors that Robinson was a painter who had studied in Europe, an unlikely story since he looked more like a backwoodsman than a painter. And the most colorful rumor of all was that the strange man was a pirate who had come to the area to escape criminal punishment. Wherever he came from, he soon became the talk of the town—especially when he started to build his magnificent mansion north of town on the banks of the Scioto River.

There weren't many fine homes at that time in the Ohio wilderness. It was the early 1800s and building materials were hard to come by.

Still, Robinson managed to get land cleared and to begin crafting a fine house.

The home he eventually built was magnificent, but it was a home that rarely had visitors. Robinson wasn't the social type. In fact, he didn't seem to like anyone. He rarely spoke to the other townsfolk and spent most of his time alone in his wonderful home. And then she came. No one knew where she had come from either—she simply showed up one day with Robinson on one of his rare visits into town. She looked barely twelve and spoke only Spanish. Her dark brown eyes looked frightened, especially when Robinson spoke to her.

Soon the folks of Delaware were all talking about the timid young girl who seemed to be living with Robinson in his mansion. Most of them assumed that she was a relative—a daughter or a niece. There were some who said that she was Robinson's indentured servant and that she was forced to wait on him hand and foot until she earned her freedom. Those who believed that Robinson was a pirate claimed that he had kidnapped her on one of his many raids. The folks who believed that Robinson was a painter thought she had been brought to Robinson's estate for one purpose—to model for his oil paintings.

The young girl soon became a familiar face around town. She ran errands for Robinson. And many hunters saw her simply roaming through the woods along the river. In the late summer sunlight, she often sat atop a rocky cliff and watched the river below her. She seemed lonely and timid in town, but those who saw her on her solitary walks along the river reported that she was strangely at peace, as if the natural world were her rightful home.

As summer faded and the trees turned golden brown, she was seen less often in the woods or on her special cliff. On her visits into town, which were becoming rarer and rarer, she seemed more nervous than she had been. Soon she stopped coming altogether. In fact, through the winter months, neither she nor Robinson were seen at all. And, in the spring, the two did not reappear in town. No one saw the young girl on the banks of the Scioto River either.

As spring blossomed into summer, the townspeople became more and more curious about what was going on at the Robinson mansion. Perhaps he had imprisoned the young girl there, they whispered. Maybe he had killed her and he was hiding the fact. Soon the townspeople were overcome with curiosity and concern for the young girl. Four men came together one afternoon, determined to pay Robinson a call and to get to the bottom of whatever was going on.

They made their way through the woods to Robinson's mansion, shouting warnings as they went. But as they came closer to the house, they realized that it was unlikely anyone was there. Thick ivy covered the windows. Weeds had taken over the yard and a family of raccoons had moved in under the porch. A large tree, the victim of a spring storm no doubt, had fallen on one side of the house.

The men knocked on the door, knowing they wouldn't get an answer. Then they used a large rock to knock the front door down. Inside, there was no sign of life. Each room was beautifully furnished and the furniture and knickknacks were completely undisturbed. It appeared as if Robinson and the young girl had simply left the mansion to spend the winter and spring elsewhere.

And then the men entered the library. It looked as if a horrible battle had been fought there. Tables and chairs had been overturned. Books had been thrown all over the place. Canvases and easels lay in heaps on the floor, some of them ripped and torn or splattered with paint.

Amid the rubble, they saw a sight that made the blood run cold in their veins— bloody handprints, first on the floor and then heading up the wall. They seemed to be leading to one painting that still hung above the fireplace. It was a painting of the young Spanish girl standing on her special rocky cliff along the banks of the Scioto River. It was as breathtakingly beautiful as the young girl herself.

The men stared at the portrait in awe of its magnificence. It seemed so incredibly life-like. The girl's deep black eyes seemed to shine with unshed tears. And her mouth looked as if it might just break into a mournful sob.

And then suddenly, the men heard something. It was horrible, wracking sobbing. And it was coming from the portrait. The portrait was actually coming to life!

The four men turned quickly and ran as fast as they could from the room, out the front door of the house, and through the woods. As they did, it seemed as if the sobbing followed them, echoing through the willow trees. They ran harder and faster through the woods, toward the river, toward town, hearing the agonizing sobbing in their ears each step of the way.

It was only when they passed the rocky cliff, the young Spanish girl's favorite perch, that the sobbing finally stopped.

No one saw the Spanish girl or the mysterious John Robinson again. And the mansion fell into further disrepair, since no one dared to visit it. Most of the folks along the Delaware and Franklin County line assumed that Robinson had murdered the beautiful young maiden and then had once again fled. Her body was never found, although after the stories the men told of the strange portrait, no one tried very hard to look for it.

The Robinson mansion eventually burned to the ground, and whatever secrets it held were lost in the fire. The portrait went up in the blaze, too, but its loss did not seem to put the spirit of the Spanish girl to rest.

There are those who still report seeing her ghostly figure roaming the banks of the river or sitting on the rocky cliff. And on early spring days, her pitiful sobbing can still be heard mingling with the rush of the water in the river.

THE
PHANTOM
SISTER

*L*OVE is the world's most powerful emotion. It is both the source of incredible joy and terrible pain. It pulls people together and tears them apart. It has been known to be the cause of murder, revenge, and even great war. But is love powerful enough to make the dead come to life?

That's exactly what happened one late afternoon in Clapham, England. It was an afternoon of terrible tragedy and intense terror. But in a strange way, it was also an incident *that provided a sense of comfort between the living and the dead.*

Mary didn't really understand why her sister Ellen had been sent away from her family's home in Clapham, England. She had heard the adults talk, of course. In deep tones, they spoke of an unsuitable man—a commoner—whom Ellen had been involved with. After all, this was nineteenth century England and Ellen was born of noble blood. It would simply not do for her to marry or even to have a romance with a commoner.

And so, on her father's orders, Ellen left one day. Mary still remembered how she looked, her eyes puffy and red, as she awaited the coach that would take her to Brighton By the Sea. Ellen's father hoped that by sending her there, she would forget about her unsuitable boyfriend.

But Mary knew that Ellen wouldn't do that. Ellen was a stubborn and loyal girl, and her feelings ran deep. Mary knew that Ellen would rather die than give up her sweetheart. And somehow Mary was struck by a painful feeling that she would never see Ellen again.

Mary brightened a bit when Ellen had

hugged her and whispered, "We'll meet again soon, little sister. Don't you fret. I promise you, I'll be back."

Maybe this will all blow over after all, Mary thought to herself. Maybe Ellen would be home from Brighton soon, a new woman, cured of her deep and stubborn passion. Maybe everything would be all right in their household once again. After all, Ellen never broke a promise.

All these thoughts tumbled through Mary's mind as she sat in her special place in the garden just after tea on a sunny afternoon. Mary loved her special place behind a row of hedges and peony bushes. There, she could see the garden and all of its visitors, but no one could detect her presence.

Then, through the prickly branches of the bushes, Mary saw an image that made her heart leap. There was Ellen, walking on the path between the rose bushes, back after just two short weeks. She was wearing her dark blue cloak, the one that mother had given her last Christmas. Below the cloak's hood, Mary could see her gentle golden curls. It was Ellen all right! She was back just as she had promised.

Mary stood up and called over to her mother,

who was seated on a bench underneath a willow tree.

"Mother, it's Ellen! She's come back!"

Her mother raised her arms in shock when she saw the figure of Ellen. "Hurry, child, "she called to Mary. "Go and greet her and then tell her to be on her way back to Brighton in a hurry. If her father finds her here, there's no telling what he'll do. I'll run to the livery and get a carriage prepared. Tell her I will see her after that."

Mary did as she was told and ran towards Ellen in her flowing blue cloak. *It is too bad Ellen will have to return so soon*, Mary thought, *but at least I have a chance to see her.*

"Ellen!" Mary called as she approached the figure. "It's so good to see you, but why did you come back? You know how father can be!"

Ellen did not answer. She turned toward Mary, and Mary noticed that Ellen's face seemed frozen in satisfied, knowing kind of smile.

"Ellen! Answer me! What are you doing here?"

Still, Ellen did not respond. Her eyes didn't even flicker with recognition as she gazed at Mary. She just stared blankly as if she was in a trance.

Mary reached up to take Ellen's hand, desperately hoping that her touch would somehow get Ellen to respond.

But as she reached for Ellen's hand, she felt nothing. She reached farther up to take hold of Ellen's arm, but her hand seemed to pass right through it. It was as if there was no flesh, no bone, only Ellen's image.

Then her hand did begin to feel something. The air where Ellen's image was standing was cold, icy cold. Though the sun was shining down, the air between them chilled Mary to the bone.

And Mary felt something else too. It was the same feeling she had felt the day that Ellen had left the house—only it was stronger. It was a feeling of certain dread. It was the sensation that something horrible had happened, something that Mary was incapable of changing.

As Mary stood trembling from fear, her teeth chattering from the cold, the figure of Ellen turned away and faded completely from view.

Mary was rooted in place for a few seconds, too terrified to move. Then she took off at full speed toward the livery where her mother had just gone.

She found her mother watching the stable

boy hook up the carriage and spilled out her terrifying tale.

"Mother," she said after she had finished telling her everything. "The worst part of it is that I know that something terrible has happened to Ellen, something neither you, nor I, nor Father can stop. In fact, I know that it's already happened. And we'll never see my dear sister again."

Mary threw herself into her mother's arms and sobbed uncontrollably. Her mother could offer no comfort. She, too, felt that the image of Ellen portended great tragedy.

It wasn't until the next day that Mary and her Mother would discover how right they were. A messenger knocked on the door of the manor house late the next day with the terrible news.

The previous day, at the precise moment that Mary had seen and spoken to her sister's image, Ellen had thrown herself off a rocky cliff in Brighton and drowned.

And even though Mary missed her sister terribly, she took comfort in one simple thing— Ellen had kept her promise. She had met Mary once again before she carried out her own tragic death.

THE DAUGHTER'S MIDNIGHT VISIT

WHY do ghosts of children haunt the living? Some say that because they died so young, the children simply want to have some fun, to continue to play among the living. Other theories claim that these young ghosts need to realize their dreams of childhood. There are those who say that young ghosts come back to warn the living of some impending danger. Still other ghost experts claim that ghostly youngsters are simply trapped in our world and have no choice *but to walk among us.*

But in Philadelphia in the 1800s, a young doctor came face-to-face with the ghost of a child who had another another mission—an urgent mission of terror and mercy.

The knocking began at midnight, just after Dr. Murphy had settled down in his warm bed. A wicked winter storm raged outside and the wind whipped through the streets of nineteenth-century Philadelphia, making a furious roar. Even through the roar, Dr. Murphy could hear the knocking. At first he tried to ignore it, but it just became louder and louder.

Finally, he wrapped himself in his coat, put his overshoes on, and answered the door.

He was surprised when he discovered the source of the loud knocking. At his front door, stood a small girl, not more than eight years old. Her light blue dress was little protection against the blizzard's whipping wind, but she seemed not to notice the cold. On her feet were a pair of battered shoes, so holey that they couldn't have provided much warmth against the icy ground. But the girl didn't seem to notice the frigid air. The only real pain or discomfort Dr.

Murphy saw was in her eyes. Her eyes held a kind of urgent sorrow, and they touched Dr. Murphy to the very depths of his soul.

"Please, sir!" the girl said in a weak and shaky voice. "You must help my mother!"

"Your mother?" Dr. Murphy asked. "Where is she? Is she ill?"

The girl only nodded and took his hand. Dr. Murphy could barely feel the weight of her hand in his as she led him through the dark, snow-covered streets.

Dr. Murphy didn't know what to make of it. What kind of mother would send a little girl out in a storm like this, even if she *was* ill? Why was the child dressed so lightly in the dead of winter? Where was she leading him? He didn't like the idea of being led into the ghettos of Philadelphia at this hour, but in spite of his uncertainty about the girl and the situation she was leading him into, he did know one thing— he felt a strong desire to help her. And every time she turned her face to him and he looked into her deep and sorrowful eyes, he knew he had no choice.

She led him through a maze of frozen streets, but never seemed to shiver against the cold night air. Finally, the two stopped in front of a broken-down apartment building. Once there, she led him down a set of ice-covered steps to the basement apartment.

It wasn't much of an apartment really, more like a dark and dingy cellar. And inside, on a bed of small and dusty blankets, a young woman lay, her forehead sweaty with fever. She moaned. Then her body was wracked by a horrible, guttural cough.

The doctor didn't need to do much more to make the diagnosis. The woman was suffering from pneumonia and was near death. Without looking back, the doctor went about his work quickly. He knew the woman would have a rough couple of days ahead of her, but she would probably make it. And she definitely would *not* have lived had she not received treatment when she did.

Before she fell into a deep and healing sleep, the woman croaked to the doctor, "How did you know to come to me?"

"It was your daughter," the doctor answered. "She led me to you," he said pointing to where he had last seen the little girl in the light blue dress.

Only the girl wasn't there.

"But my daughter," the women's voice was choked again, this time by a sob. "She had the same disease and she—well, she didn't make it. She died two weeks ago today—at the very stroke of midnight."

Dr. Murphy was sure the woman was still delirious from the fever. There had been a little girl, and she was very much alive. He had just seen her a minute ago. And she had been dressed in a blue shift and worn, torn, holey shoes. The woman must be hallucinating.

"Ah, my dear lady, you rest now. You are surely mistaken."

"No," the woman insisted, the tears now streaming down her face. "She's with the angels now. She was so sick. I went to find a doctor, but no one would come here. By the time I got home, she was gone."

The doctor sighed, and stroked the woman's hand sympathetically. "It couldn't be so. I just saw her . . ."

"All I have left of her," the woman continued, "is her dress, the one she was wearing when she died. And her shoes, not much good to anyone they were so worn. I sold her body to a medical school for research. I couldn't afford a funeral, and I needed the money. But the dress and the shoes—I still have them. They're in the closet, there . . ."

Dr. Murphy walked to the wardrobe that she pointed to, more to satisfy her than anything.

But when he opened the door to the closet, he felt his heart choke with terror.

There, in the closet, hung the same light blue dress the little girl had been wearing. And, on the floor underneath, were the worn and holey shoes.

THE GHOSTLY SWIMMER OF LAKE MICHIGAN

WHAT camp-out would be complete without a ghost story? After all, every summer camp and family campground has its own ghostly tale. At summer camps, experienced campers love to tell the stories to new campers to scare them. And for many families, telling ghost stories around a blazing campfire is part of the fun of camping together.

The ghost stories aren't true ghost stories, of course. Or are they? In Michigan, campers tell *the tale of Minna Quay, whose ghost seems to haunt Lake Michigan's icy waters. Her ghost has been seen calling for help from the waters of the mighty lake at several campgrounds and camps. And her cries always spell terror for any person who actually tries to save her.*

Sarah Hutchinson loved to go camping with her family. In her opinion, there was nothing better than loading up the family's camper with good food and sturdy gear and heading out to different campsites. It was something she and her parents did every weekend in the summer.

One weekend, her family headed to a campground right along Lake Michigan's shore. The campsites themselves were located in the woods behind some low sand dunes. It was dark when they got there, and Sarah's mom and dad started setting up the trailer and getting the campsite ready. Afterwards, Sarah knew, the three of them would gather around the campfire and tell a few ghost stories before they snuggled into their sleeping bags. It was a family camping tradition—like s'mores and early-morning walks.

What Sarah wanted to see first, though,

was Lake Michigan. She had camped alongside a number of small lakes and rivers, but she had never been to one of the Great Lakes or to the ocean. She couldn't wait to see water so wide that she couldn't see to the other side.

As Sarah's parents set up the trailer, Sarah scurried over a small dune and headed down to the beach. It was everything Sarah imagined it would be. The lake shimmered before her like dark purple silk. A slight breeze brushed against her face and stirred just a few white-caps up on the water. The air smelled clean, with just a hint of pine. It was incredible!

Sarah stared out at the expanse of blue before her. No matter how hard she squinted, she couldn't see to the other side. Somewhere out there, she knew, there were islands, some small, some large. Native Americans and French trappers had used those islands as temporary homes years ago. Today, some were rustic tourist sites. At school she had learned that hundreds of ships had sunk in Lake Michigan's waters as they traveled inland from the Atlantic ocean to the ports of Gary, Indiana, and Chicago, Illinois, and back again. These waters weren't always as calm as they seemed tonight. They could become stormy and treacherous, even to experienced sailors.

As she looked out over the water, she saw something or someone just beyond the edge of a fishing pier. It almost looked as if someone was swimming out there. But who would be swimming at this time of night?

Suddenly, she heard an urgent call break through the night air. "Help!" a young girl's voice boomed over the lapping of the waves. "Help me! I'm drowning!"

Sarah looked around. There was no one in sight to help her or the young girl.

"Please!" the girl screamed. "You have to come quick . . ." Her voice seemed to fade away and Sarah could tell she was in big trouble. There wouldn't be time to run back to the campsite to get her parents. She had to find a way to help the girl—and quickly.

Sarah knew a little bit about water safety from the class she had taken at her local pool back home. She climbed on the pier and ran to the end of it, looking from side to side for something that floated that the girl could grab on to.

"Hurry!" Sarah heard as she got to the end of the pier.

Now Sarah could see that the girl wasn't as young as she thought—in fact, she was about eighteen or so. Her long hair floated in the water like seaweed as she sank just beneath the surface.

"Oh, my gosh," Sarah said out loud. "What should I do?"

Again, she looked for something that floated to throw to the girl or for a long stick that she could use to pull her in. Even a fishing pole would work. But there was nothing on the pier.

The girl surfaced once again.

"Please," she gurgled. "You have to come in and get me out."

Again, her voice faded out as she sank beneath the surface.

Sarah knew she had to act—and act fast— or the young girl would die. But she didn't swim all that well, certainly not well enough to save a girl of her size.

"Come and get me . . .," the girl said one more time, her mouth barely breaking the surface of the water.

Sarah knew she had no choice. She slipped her shoes off so they wouldn't weigh her down. Then she bent her knees and braced herself for what she knew would be freezing cold water underneath her.

Just as her feet were ready to push off the rough wooden pier, she felt something on her shoulder. A hand! Gasping, she turned around and looked directly into the face of a young man wearing a lifeguard's T-shirt.

"Thank goodness!" Sarah said. "There's a girl out there and she's drowning!"

The lifeguard tightened his grasp on her shoulder. "No," he said. "Don't move."

"What do you mean, 'don't move'? She needs our help!"

Just then, the girl surfaced one last time. Then she sank beneath the dark water.

"Are you crazy? She needs our help. She'll die."

"She won't die," the lifeguard said.

"Why not?" Sarah asked, her voice trembling with frustration.

"Because she's already dead. Follow me back to the beach and I'll tell you the whole story."

Sarah was now totally confused. Should she go with the lifeguard? He was a stranger, after all. Or should she run back to the campground and get her parents' help? It didn't take her long to decide. She turned and ran across the beach, up the small dune and over the other side, to the the wooded campsite.

Sarah spilled out her story quickly to her shocked parents. She could tell by the look on their faces that they believed her. There was only one thing to do, they all agreed—go back to the pier and try to find the girl.

The three of them started up the dune to the beach. Just as they reached the top, a dark figure loomed above them, blocking their path.

It was the lifeguard. "Wait!" he said. "There's something you don't understand. That young girl is no young girl."

"What? I don't understand," Sarah's mother said.

"Yeah, what is this?" her dad echoed.

"She's a ghost," he said in a deep voice. "The ghost of Minna Quay. She haunts these waters."

"A ghost," Sarah said in disbelief. "Come on. She seemed so real and she really needs our help."

"That's one of her tricks," the young man said. "You see, Minna's boyfriend was a sailor who was lost in these waters back in the 1800s. When Minna heard the news, she was devastated. She couldn't imagine living without her only true love. And so she drowned herself one cold winter night. She jumped off the pier and drowned herself right there, in that very spot."

"Look here, young man," Sarah's father said. "There may be a girl out there who is in serious trouble. We don't have time for crazy ghost stories."

"This is no ghost story. This one is true. Minna plays a particularly dangerous game. She screams for help. And then she drowns those who try to help her to safety."

"This story can't be true," Sarah's mom said. "What proof do we have?"

The lifeguard just shook his head sadly. "You see," he said, his voice cracking just a bit. "I know it's true. I know it's true because I was her last victim."

With those words, he turned and walked toward the water. Just as he reached the lake's edge, his image slowly faded into mid-air.

Sarah broke out in a cold sweat. She reached out and hugged her mother and father, suddenly realizing how close she had come to losing her life in the icy waters beyond her.

It was a ghost story Sarah's family would never tell around the campfire. It was a ghost story that was just too real.

THE
CURSE
OF THE
GLOWING
BOY

*STORIES of "glowing boys," ghostly images
that seem to be surrounded by a strange and
eerie light, have been reported throughout
Europe for centuries. Some think these appari-
tions are simply ghostly beings that take on the
form of boys. Others, though, are convinced that
the images are the ghosts of actual boys who
were murdered at the hands of their parents.
Whatever they are, they seem to bring with
them a horrible curse. The sighting of a glowing*

boy is always a warning that some horrible and evil misfortune will follow.

Perhaps the most famous glowing boy story comes from nineteenth-century England. In this tale, Captain Robert Stewart seemed to be able to resist the glowing boy's evil curse—at least for a while. The horrible curse would eventually overtake him, and his bloody fate was worse than he ever would have imagined.

Captain Robert Stewart hated to admit it, but he had no idea where he was. He didn't know how he'd managed it. He knew his way well through the woods in this part of Ireland. After all, he had hunted here countless times for all kinds of game. But now, Captain Stewart was lost, hopelessly lost. And it seemed that the harder he tried to get his bearings, the more lost he became.

The storm brewing beyond the hills didn't help much. The sky had turned as black as night. Angry lightning cracked against it and thunder boomed and echoed right behind. The tree and bushes, where once he thought a fox had been hidden, now looked menacing, as if they might reach out and grab him.

The sky above him roared. Captain Robert had to find shelter—and soon—or he would be at the fate of the terrible storm. He kicked his horse's side and headed, once again, through the thick trees and underbrush hoping, praying, to find some kind of shelter, maybe a hunting lodge or even a cave.

The rain was pelting him furiously and the sky flashed an eerie yellow glow. He kicked his horse again, and his steed took him swiftly through the thick forest.

Suddenly, just ahead of him, a hunting lodge appeared. It looked like more than a lodge, actually. It seemed as if it was a country estate of some kind. It had huge turrets on either side of the entrance. The entrance itself was a solid wooden door with weathered brass fixtures. It was an impressive building, the kind Captain Stewart himself wanted to own some day, but he knew there was little chance of that. His older brother would inherit all of his father's wealth and, since the two had not spoken for years, Robert didn't expect to see a penny of the fortune.

Robert slowed his horse and dismounted. Then he ran through the rain toward the house and pounded on the huge wooden door. "Please, someone, answer!" he cried out.

And someone did answer—a nobleman from the looks of his clothing. And behind him was a small crowd of people—other victims of the storm, the host explained. He asked Robert in and invited him to sit next to the fire. There he sat inside the magnificent house and warmed himself. As he listened to the stories of the others, all who had become lost in the same woods during their travels, he couldn't help but imagine what it would be like if he owned a grand house such as this one. To be a rich nobleman—that was what Robert longed for most.

Before long, Robert's cold and wet skin had dried, and he, like the rest of the crowd, was utterly exhausted. He was glad when his host instructed the butler to show him to his room. A warm bed was exactly what he had in mind.

Robert fell quickly into a sound sleep. The rain outside his window had let up a bit, pitter-pattering a sweet lullaby. The fire that the butler had lit earlier shone softly in the fireplace and was the last light Robert saw before he closed his eyes.

After what seemed like only minutes of

sleep, Robert was jolted awake by a bright light. At first he thought that the lightning had returned or that the fire had gotten out of hand. He would soon see how wrong he was.

The fire had actually gone out. And, just to the left of it, a glow had appeared. Robert sat spellbound, too terrified to move, as the glow moved closer to his bed.

Robert saw a sight that terrified him to his bones. It wasn't just a glow. It was a boy—a boy who appeared to be glowing in the darkness. The boy had long, yellow hair and was dressed in clothes that seemed to come from another time. The strange yellow light that came from his body pervaded the room. Indeed, it seemed to reach to the depths of Robert's soul.

But it was the look on the boy's face that scared him most of all. The boy was smiling, but it was an evil, hideous grin. And it was a knowing smile, the kind of smile that suggested that something horrible had happened or would happen soon.

Robert watched in terror as the glowing boy approached his bedside. He seemed unable to move away from the boy. The smile seemed to draw him in. All he could do was grasp the bedframe until his own knuckles turned white.

It came closer and closer. Then it stopped just short of the bed itself.

Robert felt a strange relief wash over him, but the feeling was short-lived. The boy raised his hand to his throat and made a slashing movement across his own neck. Three times the glowing figure made the slashing movement. Robert grabbed his throat in his terror. And then the glowing boy disappeared. At the same time, the fire in the fireplace blazed back to life.

It was as if the whole thing hadn't happened.

Robert spent the rest of the night trying to figure out whether the image he had seen had been a dream or a real phenomenon. His body shook as he remembered the boy's horrible smile. And his neck began to burn whenever he thought about the slashing movement the boy made against his neck. It had been too real to be a dream, but Robert didn't believe in ghosts.

By morning Robert was sure that he had been the victim of a hoax, a cruel and ruthless hoax. He pulled himself out of bed, his anger rising as he did. He would have a word with the master of this house. It wasn't fair to frighten guests—even a surprise guest who had not been officially invited. He would tell the nobleman a thing or two.

Robert stomped down the stairs and approached his host, his anger seething out of control. When he told the story of the glowing boy and insisted that his host had somehow engineered the whole event just to scare him, the man's face turned white.

"Which room did you sleep in?" he asked.

"The one in the south wing. It was adequate, until your cruel joke, of course. There wasn't a lot of furniture, but I didn't need much."

"The south wing?!" The man boomed, and he screamed for his butler to appear immediately.

When the butler appeared, the man railed at him for putting a guest in that room. "You know what has gone on there!" he screamed. "I've told you never to let anyone sleep there."

"But that was the only room left, " the butler insisted. "And we haven't seen him in ever so long. I lit a fire to keep him away."

The host just shook his head, his face red with anger, and sent the butler away. Then he turned to Robert and explained.

"It seems that you have seen our glowing ghost—a boy who was murdered here some years ago by his mother. He appears infrequently and, apparently, our butler thought it was safe since he hadn't been seen for some time. I do apologize. I do hope that nothing more happens."

"What do you mean, 'nothing more happens'?" Robert asked, still trying to make sense of the man's crazy story.

"Well," the gentleman explained, "the glowing boy is both a good and bad sign. It usually means that you will come into great wealth and fame. Good things will happen to you—and you will enjoy great fortune."

Robert smiled. That didn't sound so bad. He had always wanted to be rich. It did seem a bit silly, but maybe, just maybe there was something to the story. And if there was, he would soon be enjoying life as he had never before.

"But then," the man looked gravely at Robert, "just as the person begins reaping the harvest of his wealth, great tragedy strikes. Eventually, the person dies a horrible death."

Robert just shook his head. Now he knew

the story wasn't true. How could a ghost cause all of this to happen? It just didn't sound right. And he was beginning to like this place even less than he had last night. The man of the house seemed a bit strange, a bit off his rocker with his stories. By now Robert had convinced himself once again that the ghost wasn't real at all, but was some trick cooked up by the host and his butler to scare him.

He quickly excused himself, gathered his things, and left.

Just a week after he left the mysterious manor in the deep woods of northern Ireland, Robert received some tragic news. His brother had been killed in a freak sailing accident. While Robert regretted the loss of his brother, he knew what it meant for him. He would receive his father's title, the Viscount of Castlereigh, when his father died. He would become the rich nobleman he had always wanted to be.

And Robert received that title sooner than he had imagined he would. Just months later, his father died of a strange fever, leaving him his estate, his riches, and, best of all, his title. All of this would have gone to his brother had he lived. Robert had never dreamed that he might be heir to it all. But there he was. And he relished the thought of it.

Robert used his title to gain power. He became active in politics and became an influential leader. He became the Foreign Secretary of Ireland and traveled the world. But he had developed a cruel and swaggardly attitude. Few could tolerate him, and no one really liked him.

And then, just as suddenly as it had all happened, it disappeared. Castlereigh's fortunes and his wealth dwindled. He began suffering from gout and unexplained fevers. He spent his money in odd ways, squandering it on the horses, servants, and clothing. Soon, it was all gone and, with it, his own health.

He began talking in ways that others claimed were crazy. He said he saw a yellow boy and that the yellow boy had come back to haunt him. He clutched at his throat and complained of a burning sensation there. He took to wearing high collars so he could keep the yellow boy away, or so he said. He was confined to the country house, the last piece of property that he owned. Because of his strange talk of the yellow boy and his ravings about his neck, all sharp objects were taken from Robert. The servants and doctors didn't much care about him, but no one wanted to be responsible for his suicide.

It didn't work. One stormy night, Robert raved once again about the yellow boy who had glowed in the darkness of his room in that hunting lodge. Then he claimed to see him once again. The doctors gave him medicine to calm him down, and it seemed to work for a time. He appeared to be calm, although a servant reported that the man's smile had unnerved him. It was a cruel, evil grin, the servant claimed, and it scared him to his bones.

But the sight the next morning would scare that servant even more.

Robert had somehow found a pen knife and slashed his own throat in three neat lines. And, even in the throes of death, his face wore an evil, knowing smile.

THE GHOST OF THE WOLF GIRL

BIGFOOT, the Loch Ness Monster, Yeti, and the Jersey Devil—all mysterious creatures that seem to be freaks of nature. Are these creatures real or have they been invented by overactive imaginations? Either way, the possibility that they may exist has terrified both the meek and the brave of heart.

From Texas comes the story of perhaps the most mysterious creature of all—an amazing being that is part wolf and part human girl. But there is something even more frightening about the wolf girl of the Texas plains. She has been dead for over a hundred years and yet she—or her ghost—is still seen among the sagebrush and juniper scrub.

Greg didn't wanted to take his kid brother along on this hunting trip. He wanted to go by himself, with just his guide, Old Tom, for company. But Bryan begged and begged to be taken along, so Greg finally gave in. They packed up all their sleeping bags and their bows and arrows. As they packed, Greg promised Bryan that this trip would be one they would never forget. Greg knew just how to make the trip memorable—with a terrifying story, one that would scare his kid brother so badly that he would never want to tag along again. After they were all packed, they headed into the Texas wilderness with Old Tom to hunt for wild pigs, sometimes called javelinas or peccaries.

The sun was just setting as they reached their camping spot by the Devil's River. The angle of the fading sunlight turned the craggy cliffs of the West Texas desert into strange shapes.

"You've got to be tough to hunt wild pigs," Greg told Bryan as they unloaded their gear from the back of Old Tom's truck.

"Sure do," Old Tom echoed. "Nothing pretty about those peccaries a-squealing after you shoot 'em. It can get pretty bloody."

"I'm ready for it," Bryan answered. "No problem."

He doesn't know what he's in for, Greg chuckled to himself as he began to make camp. *Wait till he hears the stories Old Tom and I plan on telling.*

As it turned out, Bryan didn't have to wait long. Just after dinner, as the fire burned down, Tom cleared his voice and began a tale. The first one was an old favorite—the one about the one-armed brakeman who appeared on the train tracks and caused terrible wrecks. Then Bryan himself got into the act and told the one about the phantom hitchhiker. Greg just sat quietly and listened. He and Old Tom had saved the best story for last.

By this time, the fire had burned all the way down. The light from the full moon that was rising between the cliffs cast an eerie glow on Old Tom's face.

"How 'bout the one about old Mollie Dent's girl?" Tom began, winking at Greg.

"That's a good one," Greg answered. "'Course it may be too scary for Bryan here. Maybe we shouldn't tell it."

"Come on, please," Bryan begged.

"Well, okay," Greg said. "It seemed some time ago there was a girl named Mollie, who was pregnant, but she didn't want to be left behind when her husband came up here to Devil's River for the spring trapping season. So she followed him."

"This doesn't sound scary," Bryan interrupted.

"Just you wait, boy," Tom answered, grinning widely.

"As it turned out, Mollie was closer to having her baby than anyone figured," Greg continued. "She gave birth right here on the banks of Devil's River. Only it wasn't an easy birth and Mollie didn't survive it."

"She died shortly after—just over yonder." Tom pointed to a small juniper tree on the side of the trickle that was known as Devil's River.

"And then a storm came up," Greg said, jumping in. "A terrible storm. Mollie's husband grabbed the baby and ran as hard as he could, hoping to find shelter."

"Shelter? Back in the 1800s in these parts? What did he think, there might be a motel or something?" Bryan laughed at his own joke.

Greg didn't laugh back. Instead, he adopted a more serious and ominous tone. "Turned out there wasn't any shelter at all, Bryan—you're right about that. And Mollie's husband was struck down by lightning before he could get very far."

"Later, when a group of sheep herders from Mexico found Mollie's and her husband's bodies, they buried the two of them. But there was no sign of the baby."

"Everybody just more or less forgot about it," Old Tom said.

"Well, let's just us forget about it and go to sleep," Bryan said, his voice slightly trembling. "It's late and we need to get hunting early."

"You scared of the rest of the story?" Greg asked his brother, knowing that it was beginning to get to him.

"Oh, no," Bryan answered weakly. "Keep going, I want to hear it."

Old Tom picked up where Greg had left off. "It wasn't until fourteen years later—maybe fifteen—that anyone gave it much thought. A young sheep herder was tending to his flock in that field over there . . ."

Bryan looked in the direction Greg was pointing. He couldn't help but wince when a streak of heat lightning flashed in the sky.

"A pack of wolves attacked his sheep one night. Only they weren't all wolves," Greg continued. "One of them was a girl with long hair all over her. She was running on all fours and had strong, overgrown shoulders, just like the wolves in the pack."

"That sounds crazy—like some comic book or something," Bryan said.

"Oh, it wasn't a comic book," Old Tom said. "Folks said it was Mollie's girl and that she had been raised by wolves—and that she had turned into a sort of wolf girl herself."

"Some scouts found strange tracks," Greg continued. "They looked like hand and foot-prints with blood on them. And they followed them until they found the wolf pack and trapped the girl. Then they took her kicking and screaming back to their cabin and locked her in a bedroom."

"Kicking and screaming?" Bryan said. "If she was a wolf shouldn't she howl?"

"Oh, she howled, too," Old Tom said. "In fact, she howled so loud that the wolf pack appeared outside the cabin. Then they began attacking it, tearing apart the wood with their claws and teeth. Finally, they made a hole in the side of the bedroom big enough for the girl to escape, but not before they killed most of the horses in the corral. They tore their necks out, they did. They didn't eat them though. They just tore their throats out and left them to bleed to death."

"And they say," Greg said, adding the final touch to the tale, "that she's still around these parts, still hunting with the pack."

"Yeah, how could she be? She'd have to be more than a hundred years old—close to two hundred even."

"It's her ghost, boy," Old Tom told him. "They say it's her ghost that still roams these parts, hunting with the pack, looking for just one more kill."

Just then a wolf's lonely howl broke through the night air.

"Maybe that's her now!"

"Yeah, right," Bryan said. "Let's just go to sleep, okay?"

The fire was completely out and Greg could

tell that Bryan was truly terrified. They had told the story so well that Greg had almost scared himself. But the best part would come the next day. He and Old Tom had another surprise for Bryan—and this one was sure to scare him to death! As Greg snuggled into his sleeping bag and closed his eyes, he laughed quietly just thinking about it.

They all awoke early and ate a hearty breakfast cooked over the campfire. Greg spoke in ominous tones about the wolf girl, but Bryan just laughed it off. Then the three headed out into the brush, their bows over their shoulders, with Bryan in the lead.

All of a sudden, Greg heard Bryan scream—a horrible, bloodcurdling scream. He ran forward and looked down toward where Bryan was pointing. There, on the dusty ground, were bloody handprints and footprints as if someone had been walking on all fours. Greg looked at Bryan. He was shaking all over.

Greg burst into laughter. "Got ya, didn't we?" he said, not able to keep the hoax going any longer.

Old Tom just stood there grinning, then said, "We tried the same trick on my little brother years ago, and we got him, too! Those aren't from any wolf girl. Me and your brother made 'em last night with a little red paint. We really fooled you, didn't we?"

Gazing into his little brother's eyes, Greg almost felt sorry for him. Then he remembered how Bryan had pestered him and pestered him until he agreed to bring him along on this trip. *It serves him right,* he thought to himself. *Now let's just see if he has what it takes to hunt the wild pigs.*

Bryan, though shaken, insisted he wanted to go on the hunt, but he wanted Greg to go first this time.

Greg kept his eyes low looking for tracks. And he moved quietly listening for the sound of a wild pig, just as Old Tom had taught him. He heard a faint scuffling sound and looked at Old Tom, who nodded. Greg knew that he would bag a pig early in the day—and he was looking forward to it. The scuffling sound grew nearer and louder. Greg strained his ears hoping to hear the low snort that would confirm that a pig was heading his way.

Only he didn't hear a snort. He heard a low wail.

He raised his eyes to the spot where the strange sound was coming from. Through the brush, he saw a slight movement, a hint of brown, and then a flash of deep sable. A wolf appeared in front of him. Greg's hand trembled on his bow. He looked back at Bryan and Old Tom. Their eyes were fixed on the clearing.

He turned back and and gasped at the sight. Behind the wolves, there was another figure. It was covered with dark brown hair and crouched on all fours. When it turned toward the group, it was clear that this wasn't a wolf at all. It had a human face, even though it was covered with hair—and it was the face of a girl.

Greg couldn't move. He seemed rooted to the ground, forced to look into the glowing eyes of the creature in front of him. It opened its mouth for just a second and growled, blood dripping from its teeth. And then just as quickly as it had appeared, it faded into the long, brown Texas grass.

Greg turned and ran, ran as fast as he could, hoping that the creature wouldn't reappear and follow them. He heard Bryan and Old Tom in front of him, thundering through the Texas bush.

Suddenly, Greg tripped and fell with a thud to the ground. He looked up. Bryan and Old Tom were standing right in front of him, their mouths open in horror their eyes fixed on the bloody mess of a creature on the ground.

Greg looked down at his feet. He had tripped over a javelina, a small wild hog, just the kind he had sought to kill with a bow. Only this one hadn't been killed with a bow. This one had had its throat ripped open, exposing bloody muscles underneath. And, even though he couldn't be sure, Greg thought he heard a howl—not a wolf's howl, but a sort of scream, coming from the clearing they had just left.

The wolf girl—or her ghost—had made one more kill. And Greg was just glad that she preferred the taste of javelina to human flesh.

THE
GIRL
AND THE
GHOSTHUNTER

*C*AN the living ever really communicate with
the dead? That's a question that people
have asked throughout history. During the late
1800s and early 1900s, a group of people
known as spiritualists were convinced that they
could make this happen. Trances, spells, and
incantations were the tools they used to "speak"
to the spirit world.

The most popular way to communicate with
the spirit world was by seance, an elaborate

ceremony in which spirits were called forth. A person called a medium was generally in charge of the seance. It was the medium's job to speak the special words that would bring a spirit into the seance room. The spirit sometimes even seemed to take over the medium's body and speak to the gathering through him or her.

Were these communications with the spirit world genuine? Probably not. Most people think that many of the seances were hoaxes and that most mediums simply pretended to be overcome by a spirit. But there was one seance, not so very long ago, that convinced even the greatest skeptic. In fact, his encounter with the spirit world was so real that it changed the course of his entire life.

The moment Harry Price heard the story of the young ghostly girl named Rosalie, he knew he had an opportunity in his hands—an opportunity to make lots of money. Harry lived in the early 1900s, a time when a movement called spiritualism was at its height. People everywhere were holding seances to bring back the dead, claiming to see ghosts, and predicting the future. It was a craze that was sweeping England and the United States. And it was a craze that was making Harry Price rich.

Harry Price was a ghost hunter—a psychic researcher who claimed to be able to contact the dead. But Harry himself didn't really believe in ghosts. He was simply very good at faking. He and the mediums he worked with rigged all kinds of things to "prove" the existence of a ghost. Trap doors, closets, wires, smoke, and doctored photographs were all used to create the effect of a ghost. And occasionally a companion of Harry's would actually dress up in white garb and emerge from a hidden room, as if rising from the dead. It was a good business to be in. People wanted to believe in ghosts. What harm was there in helping prove to people that they were real?

And that's exactly what Harry intended to do when he received a note from a woman who only wanted to be identified as Madame M. According to the note the woman wrote, she had lost her daughter Rosalie to diphtheria when the child was just seven years old. Madame M, who had also lost her husband in World War I, was overcome with grief when

Rosalie died, but after a short period of time, she was comforted by an odd feeling—a feeling that her daughter were still with her. She even claimed to hear her daughter call out to her in the dark of night. Sometimes she thought she heard her daughter weeping just beside her bed. One time, she felt her daughter's hand reach up and take hers. The note asked two questions: Could Harry Price help her? Could he attend a seance that she had scheduled with a medium the following week?

Of course I can, Harry thought to himself. *For a price.* So he wrote back to Madame M and informed her of his fee and of his willingness to come. Depending on what happened, he might take Madame M on as a client and work with her (through trickery, of course) to learn more about the long-lost Rosalie.

When Harry arrived at Madame M's, he paid close attention to the details of the place, especially the seance room. He hadn't met the medium before, but he knew of her. She had a reputation for being the real thing, for truly having the gift of psychic power. It was said that she never resorted to any kind of trickery at all. She had also been known to go into dramatic trances to communicate with the spirit world. But Harry knew she had to be up to something. He also knew that no matter how good the medium was, he could do better with his own brand of magic than she could.

The seance started just as the sun set. The seance room was completely dark. Then the medium whispered, "Rosalie, Rosalie, are you there?"

There was no answer at first, but a few seconds later Harry heard a gentle crying. Then a strange, sweet smell seemed to float through the room. *Nice touch,* Harry thought. *I wonder how she came up with that one.*

Then Harry heard a shuffling sound. That was an easy one to fake, Harry knew. Sounds could be made to seem to come from almost anywhere with just a little rigging.

Then Harry felt something touch his hand in the darkness. It felt, strangely enough, like a child's hand. But it was icy cold.

Harry's hand trembled against the icy cold one. Was this another one of the medium's clever tricks? If so, it was quite good.

Harry swallowed hard. He had to try to find out how she had pulled this one off, no matter how frightened he was. He tried to pull his hand from the icy grip, but he could not pull it free. With his other hand shaking, he reached up to feel what was in front of him.

First he felt hair—long hair, shoulder-length. Then he felt a girl's shoulders, then a starched, lacy pinafore. He gasped in terror. The girl's grip on his hand was becoming tighter and tighter. And, although he could see nothing else in the darkness, he did see a pair of glowing red eyes, eyes that were evil to their core. The pleasant smell in the room had now turned acrid. If this was the ghost of Rosalie, she meant him great harm.

Harry could have written all of these effects off to trickery, except for what happened next. He felt something brush against his ear. Then he heard the whisper, a cruel child's taunt, "Now do you believe?"

Henry trembled uncontrollably. Then the icy cold hand that had grabbed his let go. Harry heard the person seated to his right draw in her breath suddenly. Then, shortly thereafter, the next person in the circle screamed. It seemed that Rosalie was going from person to person, making her presence known. Finally, she came to the medium. The medium groaned and let out a slight scream. Then all of the candles in the room suddenly glowed, as if they had been lit by some unseen hand. And, as they burst into flame, Rosalie's evil presence—and the aroma she had brought along with her—seemed to disappear.

Harry Price went on to become a famous psychic researcher, known the world over for his investigation into the haunting of Borley Manor. It was said that he never resorted to trickery or hoaxes of any kind ever again.

Though he never spoke of his experience with Rosalie again and wrote about it only briefly, it was clear that Rosalie had convinced Harry of one thing—

Ghosts were real. He did believe.

THE
GHOST BOY
OF
ENSTWISTLE
CROSSING

*T*HERE'S something about the hollow wail of a train whistle and the clacking noise of the wheels as they pass over the tracks that simply inspire stories. In fact, people have told stories about trains for about as long as railroads have been around. There are legends about the mighty Casey Jones, runaway trains, train robberies, and hold-ups. There are even folk songs and poems about the train's lonesome whistles and regular rhythm.

And then there are the ghost stories. Tales are told about ghost trains—trains that appear out of nowhere and steam along invisible tracks, only to disappear into the night. Stories are told of horrible train wrecks that can be heard again and again on the anniversary of the actual accident. There are legends about those who come to warn others of impending danger along the railroad.

Perhaps the saddest story of all comes from Scotland about a small boy and a lonely signalman. It is a story of intense longing and regret. The sad account of this railroad haunting inspired the following ghostly tale.

Andrew Ackroyd had been in charge of the signal box on the Darwen-Bolton train line forever it seemed. It was a tedious and boring job, but an important one. He pulled levers that activated signals telling trains when to stop so other trains could pass on the single narrow track. He also pulled a lever to lower the gates so those on foot or traveling by horse and wagon would not step right in front of a speeding train. Andrew also made sure the tracks were clear for the occasional automobile that passed through—although there weren't many of those back in the 1930s in Scotland.

Andrew got to know most of the folks who crossed at this particular spot. They were mostly farmers traveling to or from town, or they were men driving milk trucks on their way to or from the dairy. He usually nodded to them or gave them a shy wave. Andrew rarely let his attention waver from the task at hand. If he failed to pull a lever or pulled one at the wrong time, a terrible accident might happen— an accident that would surely cost human life. Some signalmen would take breaks to chat when they knew that a train wasn't scheduled through, but not Andrew. He didn't want to risk it.

One day Andrew noticed someone new outside the dusty window just above his signal box. It was a young boy out in the fields, tossing a ball in the late afternoon sun. Every once in a while, he would take a break from his solitary game of catch to run back and forth in the small field next to Andrew's post, looking as if he didn't have a care in the world. Andrew wished he could enjoy that kind of freedom, and he longed to run after the boy to find out more about who he was and where he was from.

Andrew didn't see the boy again until the following Saturday at precisely the same time—five o'clock. Again, the boy tossed the ball for a while. Then he danced among the deep grass as he chased butterflies. As before, Andrew felt a deep longing to be free like that and, this time, he also felt something for the boy himself. Andrew had always wanted a son, but now he was middle-aged and had yet to settle down with a bride. It seemed unlikely that he would ever have a family.

It wasn't long before Andrew felt a special attachment to the boy, even though the two didn't speak. The boy came every Saturday afternoon at five o'clock to play in the fields by the signal office. And Andrew couldn't wait to see him.

As the summer melted into autumn, Andrew began to notice something different about the young boy. He seemed to look paler each time he saw him. He looked as if he was thinner, too. His bones seemed to stick out at all angles. And he didn't throw the ball with much enthusiasm any more. Instead, he tossed it up and down, slowly and sadly. Andrew hoped that there was nothing seriously wrong with the youngster. There were lots of sicknesses in these parts of the Highlands, and not many doctors. Many a child died of a simple ailment because it went untreated.

As Andrew watched the young boy walk slowly up the hill beyond the field, he made a resolution to himself. The next Saturday he would leave his post—just for a moment—and talk to the youngster. He would ask him where he lived and if his family needed anything—some food, perhaps, to help them through the winter. It was the least he could do. After all, watching the young boy had brought him such great joy.

The next Saturday, Andrew watched as the boy slowly made his way across the field toward the railroad crossing. It seemed he moved even more slowly and painfully this time. He held the ball in his hands, but he seemed not to have the energy to toss it up and down. His legs had grown more bony and his face, even at a distance, looked pale in the fading September sunlight.

Andrew checked his watch. He had half an hour before the next train was due through at 5:30. That was more than enough time to approach the boy and talk to him. Usually, there were just a couple of folks crossing the tracks at this time of the evening anyway. He could see one of his regulars—Old Bill Thompson from the dairy on his horse-drawn wagon down the way—a bit off in the distance on the dusty road. He would be back in plenty of time to put down the gate to warn Bill about the 5:30 train.

Andrew headed out of his small office and toward the field. The boy looked up at him with tired eyes as he approached. His skin looked almost white and his arms and his legs were so thin it looked as if they might break off.

"Hey there!" Andrew shouted.

The boy smiled weakly. Then he raised his hand and threw the ball. It sailed through the air slowly right into Andrew's hand.

"I was wondering, " Andrew said, squeezing the ball in his hand, "Do you need any . . . help?"

Andrew could barely finish his sentence. Something was happening to the boy, right before his very eyes.

The boy's tired eyes were turning a fiery red. And his white skin seemed to be melting right off his face. Andrew's heart raced. He wanted to run, but his feet seemed unable to move.

In just the briefest second, the boy in front

of him was transformed. Underneath his skin were muscles, dripping with dark red blood. And then the muscles disappeared. White bones gleamed underneath. In the empty eye sockets were blood-red, glowing eyes. In place of the boy stood his skeleton.

This has to be a dream, Andrew thought to himself. *A nightmare.* Andrew blinked his eyes, hoping against hope that the terrifying image in front of him would transform itself back into the boy he so enjoyed.

But it didn't. It disappeared altogether. The boy—or what was left of him—faded into thin air.

Andrew opened his mouth to scream, but nothing came out. Instead, he heard a sound as horrible as any he could imagine—the sound of a train engine chugging down the track. He looked at his watch in terror. It was only 5:15, but for some reason the 5:30 train was early and Andrew wasn't at his post.

Suddenly, he remembered something else. Old Bill from the dairy—he should be right at the crossing by now. Andrew turned and ran as fast as he could toward the signal house. He had to make it or . . .

The next thing he heard was the shrill wail of a whistle calling out a warning. But Old Bill was already on the track and he was moving slowly over it. Didn't he hear the whistle? What was wrong?

Andrew ran harder toward the signal house, but he couldn't get there in time. The next thing he heard was the sound of screeching metal and crunching wood, mixed with a horrible and hollow scream. In an instant, Andrew knew what had happened.

The train had hit Old Bill and smashed his wooden cart to tiny pieces. And it had pulled Old Bill himself underneath its churning wheels. His twisted body was pulled from the wreckage two hours later.

Andrew was wracked with guilt. He shouldn't have left his post, even for a second, but he had felt it was safe. After all, the next train wasn't due until 5:30. Who would have thought it would come early—a full fifteen minutes early? It had never happened before. After all, the 5:30 was so regular, you could set your watch by it.

And as if his grief wasn't enough, he continued to dwell on the vision he had had of the young boy. The whole thing was just too weird.

Had the boy been there or had it been some hallucination? He had no way of knowing. He still had the ball the boy had thrown him and every once in a while, he took it from his dresser drawer and rubbed his hands over the worn leather. There was nothing remarkable about the ball—only a couple of letters, H.T., scratched into it. Still, Andrew thought that it might hold a clue to the mystery of what had happened to him.

He knew that no one would believe him, so he didn't mention it to anyone. But in the darkest hours of the night, he would dream of the boy, first playing in the fields and then tossing the ball slowly in the air. That's when the dream turned into a nightmare. The boy turned into a hideous skeleton right before his eyes. Many a night, he woke up screaming, his body covered in cold sweat.

There was a short investigation into the accident and it was deemed just that—an accident. Andrew wasn't technically responsible to be at his post every second, especially if a train wasn't due through; therefore, the investigator in the case proclaimed Andrew innocent of any responsibility. It didn't make him feel much better, though, especially when he thought about Old Bill's family.

But it was the story the investigator told him after the whole thing was all over that made Andrew feel even worse—in fact, it chilled him to the core.

"Funny, isn't it, how history repeats itself?" the investigator commented.

"Sir? Whatever do you mean?" Andrew asked.

"Well, you must know about Old Bill's brother, Harold, don't you? He died the same way when he was just eight years old."

"Wwwwhat happened?" Andrew asked, although he was almost afraid to hear the answer.

"Well, it seems little Harold waited for his father every day around five to come back from town. They would play ball together for a short time in the field next to the signal box before they headed for home."

Andrew's heart skipped a beat.

"Seems one day, he saw his father coming down that dusty road and ran to meet him. Normally it would have been perfectly safe to cross the tracks at that time. But for some reason—nobody knows why—the train came early that day. A full fifteen minutes early. As the boy raced across the track to meet his dad, the train steamed through. It killed the lad. In fact, it practically skinned him alive. When they pulled him from the wreck, he was basically a skeleton. No one knows exactly what happened to cause that kind of injury, but we do know that he died at exactly 5:15 that Saturday afternoon in September. Come now," the investigator said, noticing that Andrew's face had turned white, "don't tell me you hadn't heard of him?"

"No," Andrew said, nearly in a whisper, thinking of the leather ball with the letters "H.T." scratched into it. "I hadn't heard of him—until now."

But Andrew couldn't bring himself say the words that were pounding in his head. *But I have seen him. Everyday around five o'clock. And now I understand why I couldn't help him.*

THE
HAUNTED
YOUNG
READER

THE library is usually a calm and serene place, a place where book-lovers of all ages come to discover books—and dreams. Inside each of the volumes the library holds is a wonderful adventure, an adventure that begins when the reader opens the first page.

But when one young girl discovered a particularly well-worn library book, she was in for more than a wonderful adventure. She was in for the most hair-raising experience of her life.

And it was an experience that she never, ever wanted to repeat.

There was nothing that Allison liked better than poetry. Emily Dickinson, Edgar Allan Poe, and William Shakespeare were among her favorites. But Allison not only liked to read poetry, she liked to write it, too. Her journal was filled with verses and rhymes, all written with her favorite purple pen.

In Allison's town of Greencastle, Indiana, there were two libraries. The public library, which had a wonderful children's section and a good section of poetry, and the Depauw University Library. Most of Allison's friends used the public library and Allison did, too—at least until she had checked out every single book of poetry the library had to offer. Then she began visiting the university library, where she discovered a whole new collection of books. She wasn't sure if she could check books out of the university library or not and she was afraid to ask, so she simply spent long afternoons reading in one of the library's comfortable chairs. There, she whiled away the hours reading the magical words of Rudyard Kipling,

Elizabeth Barrett Browning, and Robert Frost.

One autumn afternoon, when Allison was roaming through the poetry section, she found a shelf that she hadn't seen before, just beyond the poetry section. A sign just above the shelves read, "The Whitcomb Collection." The shelves themselves were filled with dusty books. Some had brown covers with gold-embossed titles. Others had colorful pictures on their covers. There were thick volumes and thin, small volumes. And there were books of all kinds—fiction, nonfiction, and, best of all, poetry.

Allison browsed through the books of poetry. She had already read most of the books on the shelves. Then she found a book she had never seen. Its cover was deep blue with stark, white lettering. On the cover it read, "The Poems of Oison."

Allison eagerly opened the book and turned to the book's introduction. The book explained that Oison was a poet from India whose poems told of the rich and exotic landscape of his homeland. When Allison read the first poem in the book, she understood exactly what the introduction was saying. The poem seemed to sweep her away to another time, another place.

It was a place full of wonderful and strange sensations—soft silks, rich incense and spices, flowing music, vibrant colors, and sweet and spicy foods. It was a wonderful feeling of escape.

When it was time for the library to close for the day, Allison couldn't bear to give the book up. She would keep it overnight, she decided quietly to herself as she slipped it into her backpack. No one would notice, surely. After all, she hadn't even noticed the Whitcomb Collection until that very moment.

That night, she read again the incredible poems of the man named Oison and seemed to be transported directly to India. The poems made her feel more mature somehow, as if she were old enough to actually visit the strange and wonderful place. It was as if she were traveling on a wonderful journey, a journey prepared just for her. She read deep into the night and fell asleep with the volume of poems flat against her chest.

She awoke with a start. From the other side of her bedroom door she heard heavy breathing followed by a scuffling sound. She arose trembling from her bed, the book tumbling from her chest. And just as it hit the ground, the doorknob slowly turned.

Allison gasped. In her doorway stood an old man, only he wasn't a solid figure. It was as if she could see right through him. His face was lined with deep wrinkles. His clothes looked as if they came from a different time, the early part of the century perhaps. His thin arms were outstretched, as if he were trying to grab her. His long and bony fingers reached out to her as she cowered in the corner of the bed.

Then the figure spoke. "Who stole the Oison? I want my Oison!" it said in a raspy voice.

Allison tried to scream, but nothing came out.

The figure repeated louder, its horrible bony fingers reaching toward her, "Give me back my Oison? You must give it back!"

Allison looked desperately around her room. She had to find a way out, away from this hideous vision in front of her, but the old man stood between her and the door. Suddenly, her eyes fell upon the book of poems she had been reading earlier. By the light of her reading lamp, she saw the word "Oison" in gold letters on the book's spine. It was the book he wanted. She picked it up and thrust it in front of her,

her fingers trembling.

The figure of the old man shook his head. "Take it back! Take it back!" he said, his voice firm.

And then the image grew fainter and fainter in front of her until it disappeared altogether.

As soon as Allison could muster the courage, she ran from her room to her mother's room down the hall. There, she told her the whole story—how she had taken the book without checking it out, how much she had enjoyed the wonderful poems inside, and how she had seen and heard the image of the old man in her room begging her to return the book.

Her mother just smiled at her. "I'm sure it was just a bad dream," she said. "Sometimes when we feel guilty about something, it comes out in all sorts of weird ways in our dreams. That's probably what happened to you. You felt badly about taking the book without checking it out, and this was your mind's way of resolving it."

"It wasn't a dream, Mom. I know it," Allison insisted.

Her mother just reached out to Allison and hugged her. "You can sleep in my bed tonight," she said. "And tomorrow, we'll return that book together and explain the whole thing to the librarian."

Allison didn't sleep a wink that night. The next day, at the stroke of nine o'clock, she would be at the front door with the book in her hand. She would take it back as soon as the library was opened. That would keep the awful ghost away forever.

Allison and her mother didn't talk as they rode to the library on the big sprawling college campus. Allison knew that her mother still thought she had just had a nightmare, but her mother just didn't understand how real the image had been. When they reached the library, Allison grabbed the book and she and her mother marched up the library's steps.

They approached the librarian behind the desk. Allison had hardly begun explaining what had happened when the librarian interrupted her.

"Wait just a minute," she said. "You took this book from the Whitcomb Collection?"

"Yes," Allison answered. "It was full of the most wonderful poems. I was going to return it and . . ."

"By any chance did you receive a visit from anyone last night?"

"My daughter had a nightmare," her mother answered for her. "Something about an old man wanting the book back. It must have been her guilty conscience."

"It wasn't a nightmare, Mom," Allison insisted. "There was an old man in my room—a sort of a ghost or something. And he kept saying he wanted his 'Oison' back. That's the name of the writer who wrote those poems."

"That was no nightmare," the librarian answered in a low voice.

"What your daughter saw was quite real."

"What? I don't understand," Allison's mother answered.

"You see," the librarian explained, "that book is from a collection of books that was donated to the library by James Whitcomb's family after his death. He was the former governor, you know."

"Yes, go on," Allison said, breathlessly.

"Well, it was his wish that his collection of books should stay in the library building always. Every once in a while, one finds its way out the door. They always come back, though.

Usually the very next day. You see, the ghost of Governor Whitcomb always pays a visit to whoever takes a book from his collection. And he always makes sure the book is returned to our shelves."

Allison swallowed hard. Could it have really been the ghost of Whitcomb who had visited her last night? What other explanation could there be?

"H-h-how do you know this?" Allison asked. "I mean, how can you be sure it's him?"

"Because, my dear," said the librarian, her face crinkling into a smile. "I once borrowed this book. And he came to claim it. You see, I saw him, too."

THE POLTERGEIST'S VICTIM

*I*T'S terrifying to see a ghost, but it may be even more frightening only to feel its presence. That's exactly what happens when a mysterious spirit called a poltergeist comes to visit. Objects may begin flying around the room as if hurled by an unseen hand. A piece of furniture might mysteriously move by itself. Bizarre sounds, knockings, and growlings may be heard. And the source of all of this ghostly activity is never seen.

Some studies indicate that poltergeists seem to have a special attraction to children— especially troubled children who are undergoing some kind of change in their lives. For this reason, some psychic researchers believe that poltergeists are not real at all. Instead, they feel that children themselves are causing the poltergeist activity through their own un- happiness. Others feel that poltergeists are spirits who simply prey on weak and sad youngsters. Whatever their actual identity, poltergeists have been noted throughout history and all over the world, and they are still being reported today.

One of the most terrifying accounts of poltergeist activity comes to us all the way from South Africa. This evil spirit, known as the Tokolosi, was so relentless it drove one little girl and her family from their homes.

"Poppycock!" Major Williams told his em- ployee, Andrew Stevens. Andrew had just told Major Stevens an incredible story. Andrew claimed that his very own daughter, Mary, seemed to be haunted by some invisible force. First Andrew claimed that a clod of dirt mysteriously fell from the ceiling of their house during dinner—right onto Mary's plate. They thought nothing of it at first, Andrew said, but then more strange things began to happen. When Mary drank from her cup, the cup seemed to fly from her hand. When she got up to clean up the mess, her chair flew completely across the room. And then Mary herself fell to the ground as if she had been shoved.

It all sounded ridiculous to Major Williams, and he was sure that it was just a story that Andrew was making up to explain his frequent absences from work. Major Williams had to admit that Andrew was clever. There were many stories that circulated throughout the South African countryside about poltergeists and ghosts. It was the 1920s, after all, and the world was caught up in belief in the supernatural.

Then Andrew came up with the most frightening revelation of all—the horror, he claimed, was the work of the terrible Tokolosi. Andrew said he was desperate. He needed the major's help.

Major Williams knew that many of the farm folk believed Tokolosi was an especially fearsome poltergeist. They said that the Tokolosi was relentless in the way that it worked its tragic magic. Its victims had been known to go completely mad or to commit suicide, so crazed were they by its bizarre manifestations. But Williams didn't really believe in its power, and he certainly didn't believe Andrew. Andrew was definitely making it up—but he was on to his tricks. Andrew kept raving about Mary and the evil poltergeist. He claimed that things had gotten worse from there. Mary was in a state of constant fear. Every night, she woke up screaming, claiming that someone or something was in her room. And she grew sicker and sicker with each horrible event.

Williams knew that he would have no rest— and that Andrew would continue to miss work—unless he got to the bottom of the situation. He had to prove that Andrew was making the whole thing up, so he followed Andrew one morning to his home on a farm near Georgetown in South Africa's Cape Province.

Once he arrived, the major asked to be alone with Mary. Andrew and his wife agreed, and they left to work in their small garden.

Williams bolted the door of the room from the inside and sat down. He planned to talk to Mary seriously. Maybe if she opened up a bit, she would admit that the "poltergeist" was simply a made-up monster, an excuse so that her father could find a way out of working.

Williams spoke in quiet, comforting tones to Mary and at first she seemed to be listening and responding. There were problems in the family, she said. But nothing big. And her father, she insisted, was an honest, hard-working man and always told the truth.

Then she stopped talking altogether. Her eyes seemed locked upon an image directly in front of her, but there was no image in sight. Williams sighed. This girl was certainly a dramatic actress. Suddenly, Major Williams felt something brush past his face—it was something furry, but Williams couldn't see it. A horrible and rank smell filled the room. It was so awful that it made Williams's eyes water and his head hurt. Surely this was not something Mary could make happen, he told himself, but maybe there's some other explanation.

In the very next instant, Mary screamed, a bloodcurdling scream of pure agony. She flung herself out of her bed, as if she had been thrown out by some unseeable force.

She lay sobbing on the floor.

Williams ran to the door and unbolted it. Then he flung it open. Next he opened the window. Sunlight and a fresh breeze filled the room and the horrible stench began to fade.

He reached down to comfort Mary as she lay on the floor. Then he saw something that made him pull his hand away in terror.

On the side of Mary's face were four bloody slashes, as if something with sharp claws had scratched her face. A thin trickle of blood dripped from each mark and mingled with Mary's tears.

It took some time, but Major Williams was able to comfort the young girl. Her parents arrived just after Williams had washed her wounds and cleansed her face of the tears. Mary fell into a deep and troubled sleep and Williams moved, with Andrew and Andrew's wife, into the kitchen to discuss what to do next.

Williams didn't know what to make of the terrifying encounter, but he was sure of one thing. Andrew was not making this up. Whatever was bothering Mary was in the house, he reasoned. Maybe she would be better off somewhere else—in a hospital, perhaps. Andrew had to agree. They had to get her out of here, and the sooner the better. Major Williams said he would make the arrangements and that he would come and take them away the next day.

But the following day, when Williams arrived at the family's small farmhouse, there was no trace of Mary or her mother or father. As Williams stepped inside, he smelled the traces of stench he had smelled earlier in Mary's room. It wasn't quite as strong, but even a tiny whiff sent his head reeling.

He looked around the house a bit and, at first, everything seemed in order. On the floor of the living room were folded clothes ready to put away. Breakfast was set on the kitchen table. The stove was still on and a large kettle of water bubbled on top of it.

Then Williams noticed the doors. On every door inside the house were four distinct slash marks. It was as if a creature had been trying to get to whoever was on the other side. On Mary's door, the paint had been scratched severely and the wood was practically split.

Williams's mind was suddenly filled with terrifying questions. Had the invisible creature—the Tokolosi—taken the family to his own horrible world? Had they simply left in a hurry and gone far away, where they hoped the poltergeist couldn't find them? Or had the Tokolosi driven them to a quiet and undiscovered suicide somewhere?

It was a question that would haunt Major Williams for the rest of his life. The entire family seemed to have simply disappeared from the face of the earth. He never saw them or experienced the terror of the Tokolosi again, but thereafter he never questioned the reality of the poltergeist and its power.

About The Author

There is nothing Tracey Dils likes better than a good ghost story. When she was growing up, she loved to scare her friends and family with terrifying tales of haunted places. In fact, she scared her little sister so badly that to this day she still sleeps with the lights on!

Tracey has never actually seen a ghost, but she has seen evidence of one. She was having lunch at an old inn in her hometown. The inn was said to be haunted. While she was eating, a tray of salt and pepper shakers rose off a counter, hung in midair for a few seconds, and then fell to the floor in one big crash. Traccy thinks that a ghost was trying to get her attention so that she'd write a story about it.

When she's not writing or spending time with her husband, Richard, and her two children, Emily and Phillip, Tracey loves to talk to young people about writing. She has held ghost-story writing workshops in schools, libraries, and writing centers throughout her home state.

Tracey is also the author of *The Scariest Stories You've Ever Heard, Part III*, as well as several picture books, including *Annabelle's Awful Waffle*, *A Look Around Coral Reefs*, and *Big Bad Bugs*.